WellieWishers™

The Mystery of Mr. E

By Valerie Tripp

Illustrated by Thu Thai

★ American Girl®

Editorial Development: Jennifer Hirsch
Art Direction and Design: Riley Wilkinson and Jessica Annoye
Production: Jeannette Bailey, Caryl Boyer, Cynthia Stiles, and Kristi Tabrizi
Vignettes on pages 92–95 by Flavia Conley

americangirl.com/service

Parents, request a FREE catalog at **americangirl.com/catalog.**
Sign up at **americangirl.com/email**
to receive the latest news and exclusive offers.

For Patty Holt,
with love

Meet the WellieWishers

The WellieWishers are a group of fun-loving girls who each have the same big, bright wish: to be a good friend. They love to play in a large and leafy backyard garden cared for by Willa's Aunt Miranda.

Ashlyn

Willa

Emerson

When the WellieWishers step into their colorful garden boots, also known as wellingtons or *wellies*, they are ready for anything—stomping in mud puddles, putting on a show, and helping friendships grow. Like you, they're learning that being kind, creative, and caring isn't always easy, but it's the best way to make friendships bloom.

Camille

Kendall

GARDEN MAP

Carrot's Hutch

Playhouse

Garden Gate

Aunt Miranda's House

Garden Theater Stage

Chapter 1

Wishing for Fun

Another snowy, sleety day," sighed Willa. "We'll have to play indoors."

"*Again*," griped Kendall.

"I wish something fun would happen," moped Emerson. "Something mysterious and exciting for a change."

"Me, too," said Camille. "Can anyone think of something fun to do?"

"I have an idea," said Ashlyn. "Let's put on costumes and then play a guessing game."

"Okay," said the WellieWishers, perking up. Costumes and dress-up were always fun.

In a flurry of giggles, the girls concocted costumes out of the things in the dress-up trunk. Outside, the wintry sky was still gray and drippy, as it had been day after day after day. But inside the playhouse, light from the lamp shone on the girls' costumes, making their bright colors glow and their glitter and sequins sparkle.

"I'll go first," said Ashlyn. She made up a rhyming riddle:

> Who am I?
> When you see me flutter by,
> You say, "Hello, _____ "

"Butterfly!" finished the girls.

"Yes!" said Ashlyn. Gently, she moved her arms to make her wings open and close.

"Now me!" said Willa. She said:

> I fly at night, and when I do,
> I spread my wings and hoot,
> *"Whoo-oo!"*
> Whoo-oo am I?

"You're an owl," answered the girls.

Willa spread her wings and blinked her owlish eyes. *"You-oo* are right!" she said.

"My turn!" said Emerson.

Moon on my hat,
stars on my dress.
I'm a beautiful sight.
Who am I? Can you guess?

"Are you the night sky?" asked the girls.

"Yes!" said Emerson, spinning so that the lamplight made the moon and stars on her costume flicker and shine.

"I'll go now," said Camille.

Shells and starfish live in me.
Who am I?
I am _____

"The sea!" said the girls.

"Yes, the sea, that's me," said Camille.
She curtsied, and her cape floated and
fluttered like sea plants in a gentle wave.

Kendall stepped up.

I have lots of green leaves.
I'm a treat for your nose.
I'm a beautiful flower,
I'm a pretty, red _____

"Rose!" said the girls.

"Right!" said Kendall. *"Mmmm,"*

she said as she
pretended to
smell the rose
on her stick.

"I can't wait until we have *real* roses in the garden again," sighed Camille. "It's been cold and snowy for such a long time."

"*Snow* kidding!" joked Emerson, lying on her back.

"The snow is pretty," said Ashlyn. "But I wish I could wave my wand and make it all melt."

Willa stood up and peeled off her owl mask. "What'll we do *now*?" she asked.

"Let's pretend that Ashlyn's wand *is* magic," said Camille, "and it can melt the snow!"

"And let's make up a song about all the fun things we'll do when winter is over," said Emerson.

"Okay," said Ashlyn. She waved her wand. *"Abracadabra!* Good-bye, ice and snow." Then she sang to the tune of "Old MacDonald Had a Farm":

We can go down to the pond
When the ice is gone.
Feed the ducklings and the geese,
Minnows, crayfish, swans.
With a duck, duck here,
and a duck, duck there,
Here a duck, there a duck,
Everywhere a duck, duck!
We can go down to the pond
When the ice is gone.

Emerson sang next:

We could dig a garden plot
And plant lots of seeds:
Carrots, pumpkins, melons, squash,
Lettuce, beans, and peas.

Then Camille sang:

We'll walk barefoot
With the grass
Tickling our toes!
Wade in puddles, splash in mud,
Wash off with the hose.
With a splish-splash here,
And a splish-splash there,
Here a splish, there a splash,
Everywhere a splish-splash.
We'll walk barefoot with the grass
Tickling our toes.

"It seems like winter is going to last forever," Emerson moaned.

"Really," said Ashlyn, waving her wand, "we all just wish for one thing: fun."

Just then, Aunt Miranda poked her head in the door.

"Hi, girls," she said. "There's somebody I'd like you to meet."

She opened the door wider, and . . .

A big, hairy dog bounded up to the playhouse door.

"Oh!" exclaimed the girls, stepping outside as the dog wagged its tail and licked their hands in a friendly way.

"This is Mr. E," said Aunt Miranda. "My friend Shu Ping asked me if his dog could stay here for a few weeks while he's traveling in China. Will you help me look after Mr. E?"

"*Yes!*" shouted the girls, delighted.

"Wow," said Ashlyn, looking at her wand. "Maybe my wand really *is* magic. Because our wish for fun just came true!"

Chapter 2

Taking Care of Mr. E

On a blustery afternoon a few days later, the girls were taking Mr. E for a walk, as they had every afternoon since the dog's arrival. They took turns carefully holding the leash as they walked all around the garden. They had to be patient, because Mr. E liked to sniff every rock, tree stump, soggy pile of leaves, and slushy puddle.

"Isn't Mr. E the most fun guest we've ever had in the garden?" said Camille.

"Oh, yes," agreed the girls.

When they got back to the playhouse, the girls made sure that Mr. E was dry and comfortable. Then Camille read a story aloud. Emerson scratched Mr. E's ears, and the dog's tail went *thump, thump, thump* happily.

Soon Aunt Miranda stopped by. "Hi, girls," she said. "I've brought some scarves for the dress-up trunk." She smiled. "What project are you doing now?"

"Willa's worried about the animals in the garden finding enough food to eat," explained Ashlyn. "So we're making a string of popcorn to hang on a tree for them to eat."

"We're almost all out of popcorn, though," said Willa. She fed some broken bits to Mr. E, who gobbled them up eagerly.

"I've got popcorn at my house," said Aunt Miranda. "I'll go pop some batches for you and be right back."

"Thanks," said the girls.

"Would you like to come with me, Mr. E?" asked Aunt Miranda, patting the dog on the head.

But Mr. E had curled up on the rug and was clearly too comfy to move.

"It looks like somebody wants to stay here with you girls," said Aunt Miranda. "Is it okay if I leave Mr. E here a bit longer while I go back to my house?"

"Sure!" said the WellieWishers.

"Thanks," said Aunt Miranda. "See you later, girls. You, too, Mr. E."

"I wonder what the *E* in *Mr. E* stands for?" said Camille after Aunt Miranda had left.

Willa patted the sleepy dog. "Well, I don't think the *E* stands for *Energetic*," she chuckled.

"Or *Exciting* or *Elegant*," added Emerson.

"I think it stands for *Extra lovable*," said Kendall, gently hugging Mr. E's head.

"Or maybe *Extremely sweet*," said Ashlyn.

All the girls looked fondly at Mr. E, who sighed with contentment and settled in for a nap.

Mr. E, who was never exactly a frisky dog, was especially sleepy and sluggish today, so the girls worked quietly. When they finished stringing all the popcorn they had, Kendall said softly, "While we wait for Aunt Miranda to bring us more popcorn, let's go hang up this string for the animals."

"Okay," whispered the girls. As noiselessly as possible, they bundled up in their outdoor clothes. On tiptoe, they crept past the snoring dog.

They left the door open in case
Mr. E. woke up and wanted to come
join them later.

The girls ran all over the garden. It took quite a while to find the perfect tree, but at last they did.

The WellieWishers were happily hanging the string of popcorn on the tree when Aunt Miranda returned.

"Hi, girls!" she said. "Sorry it took me so long. I popped a couple of batches of popcorn for you. Where's our dog?"

"We left Mr. E asleep in the playhouse," said Willa.

"*Hmm*, that's odd," said Aunt Miranda. "I just put the bags of popcorn inside the playhouse. I didn't see any sleeping dog in there."

"We left the door open in case Mr. E wanted to come outside," said Camille.

"Mr. E is probably wandering around the garden," said Kendall.

"Here, Mr. E!" called Ashlyn.

"Mr. E!" called all the girls. "Come!"

"Yoo-hoo!" called Aunt Miranda.
"Come on, sweetie!"

"*Wheeoh-wheet!*" whistled Emerson.

But no dog came running.

"Mr. E *must* be somewhere in the garden, because the gate is shut," said Willa. "Let's go search."

"Okay," said the girls.

"No, no," Aunt Miranda said calmly. "It's nearly dusk. It's time for you girls to go home. Mr. E will show up at my house, probably around dinnertime. Don't worry."

The girls left, but they couldn't help worrying.

As Camille said to the girls when they parted at the gate, "It just isn't like Mr. E not to come when we call."

Chapter 3

Where Is Mr. E?

The next afternoon, the worried girls went straight to Aunt Miranda's house and knocked on the door.

"Did Mr. E come home?" asked Kendall.

"Yes and no," said Aunt Miranda. "I left food and water outside last night, and this morning they're gone.

So I'm pretty sure that Mr. E came and ate and drank them."

"It could have been a raccoon," said Willa.

"There were paw prints in the snow," said Aunt Miranda, "and I think that they were a dog's."

"But then why didn't Mr. E stay at your house and bark to be let in?" asked Camille.

"I don't know," said Aunt Miranda, shaking her head.

"What if Mr. E has found a way out of the garden?" asked Emerson. "Maybe Mr. E went back to Shu Ping's house."

"I went over to Shu Ping's house today," said Aunt Miranda. "It's closed up, but I looked all around outside and did not find Mr. E. There were no paw prints either."

"Oh, I hate to think of Mr. E sleeping outside in the cold," said Ashlyn, shivering in sympathy.

"Well, just in case Mr. E left the garden, we'll make Missing Dog signs to put up all around the neighborhood," said Kendall.

"That'll be good," said Aunt Miranda. "I've already e-mailed my neighbors, alerted the police, and called all the animal shelters in town. If anyone finds Mr. E, we'll know soon."

"Meanwhile, we'll search the whole garden today," said Willa.

But the girls didn't find Mr. E in the garden, and no one called Aunt Miranda to say that they'd found Mr. E that day, or the next day, or the day after that.

Still, the dog food that Aunt Miranda left outside disappeared every night, and there were fresh paw prints in the snow by the bowls every morning. So the girls and Aunt Miranda were almost certain that Mr. E was in the garden—at least *some* of the time.

On the fourth day, as they had every day, the determined girls searched the garden high and low, from one end to the other. It was tough. Their feet slipped on the snowy ground. Sometimes they fell and snow got in their wellington boots and melted. Snow stuck in clumps on their mittens, plopped off branches onto their heads, and trickled icily down their necks. They shouted and hooted and hollered for Mr. E until their throats were sore.

They found a few paw prints here and there, but the wind blew the wispy, whiskery snow all around, so that any tracks Mr. E might have left were covered.

No matter how hard they tried, the girls could not find the dog in the garden.

Mr. E!

"I just don't understand why we can't find Mr. E," said Ashlyn, stamping and stomping to get the snow off her boots. "We know he has to be in the garden somewhere."

"Yes," said Camille, "because the gate is always closed. There's no way out."

"We know that he comes to the garden when he's hungry," said Kendall, "because the food and water that Aunt Miranda leaves out disappears every night."

"A raccoon could be eating it," Willa pointed out again.

"Aunt Miranda thinks that the paw prints around the bowls are a dog's," said Camille.

"But if Mr. E is in the garden, why doesn't he come when we call?" asked Ashlyn.

"Maybe he can't hear us," said Kendall.

"Or maybe he's hurt and can't come," said Willa in a small, sad voice.

"Or maybe he just doesn't *want* to be found," said Emerson.

"Why not?" wailed the other girls.

"Don't ask me," Emerson shrugged. "It's a mystery."

The next day, there was a *new* mystery.

"Look at this mess," wailed Kendall. "Some animal got into the playhouse and ate a bunch of the popcorn."

"Maybe it was Mr. E," said Camille.

"Or maybe it's the raccoon that might be eating the dog food Aunt Miranda leaves out," said Willa.

"Do raccoons steal costumes?" asked Emerson. "Because one of the costumes is missing."

"Gosh!" said Ashlyn. "It seems like there's a thief in the garden."

"*No!* Don't say that," cried the girls.

"Well, there may not be a thief," said Kendall, "but there's definitely a *mystery* in the garden."

"Yes," said Camille. "It's a mystery called *Why Are Things Disappearing*?"

The girls went to work cleaning up the playhouse. It was a warm and sunny day, so Willa opened the door to sweep popcorn crumbs outside for the animals to eat.

Plip.

"Look," said Willa. "The snow is melting, just as we wished for!"

All the girls crowded in the doorway to look. The sun shone hot and strong in the bright blue sky. It turned the drops of dripping snow into prisms and it melted the glittery snow into slush.

"The ice is going away at last," said Emerson. She sang to the tune of "Old MacDonald Had a Farm":

With a drip, drip here,
And a drip, drip there,
Here a drip, there a drip,
Everywhere a drip, drip!

"We should celebrate," said Ashlyn, who loved parties.

"Celebrate?" said Kendall. "I don't really think any of us is in a party mood." She listed the reasons on her fingers. "Mr. E is gone. The popcorn for the animals is gone. A costume is gone. And soon the snow will be gone—which means that time is passing and Shu Ping will be coming back from China."

The girls were quiet. Then Camille said aloud what they were all thinking, with sinking hearts. "Pretty soon, Aunt Miranda will have to let Shu Ping know that Mr. E is gone."

"No, no, no!" said Ashlyn. "Mr. E is only *lost*. We just haven't found him yet. We shouldn't give up and say that he's *gone*."

"Ashlyn's right," said Emerson.

"Giving up would just make Aunt Miranda—and all of us—feel worse."

Willa put on her coat and hat. "We can't do anything about Shu Ping returning soon," she said briskly, "but we *can* do something to make Aunt Miranda and ourselves feel better. We can—"

"*Find Mr. E!*" exclaimed the girls.

"He's *got* to be in the garden," said Kendall. "It's up to us to find him."

Chapter 4

Mr. E Mystery

Carrot wanted to come along, so Camille scooped him up and carried him in her arms as the girls set off to search the garden one more time.

The melting snow was so slippery under their wellies that walking up the hilly part of the path was a bit like doing the Bunny Hop: For every step forward, they slid back two. It was so warm that the girls soon shoved their scarves, hats, and mittens into their pockets and unzipped their coats. By the time the girls got to the top of the hill, they were sweaty.

"I'm roasting," moaned Ashlyn, flopping onto a big rock. "Can we rest for a second?"

Kendall nodded. She was too out of breath to talk.

Camille put Carrot down and flapped the sides of her coat to fan herself.

"It's nice to have this bare rock to rest on," said Willa. "This is the first day since we started searching that it hasn't been covered with snow."

Kendall sighed. "That's the only difference between today and every other day," she said. "Just like always, we've looked and looked but we haven't found Mr. E."

All the girls were sadly silent. They knew that Kendall was right.

Ashlyn turned to Camille. "Bless you," she said.

"I didn't sneeze," said Camille.

"Oh," said Ashlyn. "I heard a teeny sneeze, and I thought it was you."

"I heard a sneeze, too," said Willa. "I guess it was Carrot."

"Do bunnies sneeze?" asked Kendall.

"Sure they do," said Willa. "Where *is* Carrot, anyway?"

"Right here," said Emerson. She picked up Carrot to show him to Willa.

Suddenly, *floop*! Carrot jumped out of Emerson's arms and hopped—hip, hop, hippity—to the other side of the big rock.

"Hey!" said Emerson. "Where are you going, Carrot?"

The girls slid off the rock and
followed the bunny. Carrot's ears
stuck straight up and his nose quivered
as he stared into a little cave under the
overhanging rock.

The girls peered in to see what
Carrot was looking at.

There, curled up cozily, was Mr. E
and . . .

"Puppies!" breathed the girls, enchanted.

"Oh, Mr. E," said Willa. "We are so glad to find you. And your puppies are *so* cute!"

"Now we understand why you disappeared," said Ashlyn. "You came to Aunt Miranda's house and the playhouse to get food, but you had to come back to your beautiful little puppies."

"They're *wonderful*," said Emerson. "I *love* them."

"I bet we passed this little cave a hundred times," said Kendall, "but it was hidden by the snow. Thank goodness the snow has melted, so we could find Mr. E."

"I'm going to get Aunt Miranda," said Emerson, already zooming down the hill. "We'll be back in a flash."

"Tell her we found Mr. E," Camille shouted after her. "But keep the puppies a surprise!"

In no time at all, the girls saw Aunt Miranda running up the hill.

Her hair was windblown and wild,
and she wasn't wearing a coat.
Emerson was right on her heels.

"Mr. E!" Aunt Miranda called as she
came. "Oh, I've been so worried about
you!"

Aunt Miranda squatted to look into the cave. When she saw the puppies, she gasped, fell back, and sat down hard—*thud*—on the wet, muddy ground. "Puppies?" she squeaked.

The girls laughed with joy.

"Five!" announced Kendall.

"Aren't they the cutest things you've ever, ever seen?" asked Ashlyn.

"Yes," said Aunt Miranda. Softly, Aunt Miranda stroked the dog's head. "I'm proud of you, sweetie," she said.

"Wait a second," said Willa. "How did Mr. E have puppies? Isn't he a boy?"

Aunt Miranda grinned. "Did you say *Mr. E*?" she asked. "I guess you've never seen the dog's name written down, have you? Her name is Mystery, not Mr. E. She mysteriously appeared at Shu Ping's house one day. He tried to find out who her owner was, but he never could. So she became Shu Ping's dog, and he named her Mystery."

"Mystery has solved the mystery of the disappearing food," said Ashlyn.

She held up a popcorn bag. "Mystery took it to eat!"

"Mystery took the costume, too," said Emerson, pointing to a bedraggled cloth on the ground. "But I guess she needed it to keep her puppies warm, so we don't mind."

Aunt Miranda held her hand out, and Mystery licked it lovingly. "Will you trust us to carry your puppies home, Mystery?" asked Aunt Miranda.

Mystery licked her hand again.

"I think that's a yes," said Aunt Miranda.

So, very, very gently, each girl picked up a squirmy puppy, and then very, very slowly walked down the hill. Mystery circled them, keeping a watchful eye, as Aunt Miranda led them all to her house.

Once inside Aunt Miranda's house, Mystery seemed impatient and a little nervous. But she sighed happily when she and her puppies were safely settled in her comfy bed. Soon the whole darling, doggy bunch had fallen asleep.

"Oh, it is going to be so sad when Shu Ping takes Mystery and her puppies away," said Camille.

"Aunt Miranda," asked Willa, "do you think if Shu Ping agrees we could keep the puppies here in the garden?"

"No, honey," said Aunt Miranda gently. "Five puppies in a garden would be too much. They'll dig up the flowers and vegetables, and scare the birds and animals, too."

The girls knew that Aunt Miranda was right. Still, they couldn't help being heartbroken.

"We'll miss them terribly," said Kendall, brushing away a tear.

"Because we already love the puppies as much as we love Mystery," said Emerson, "and that's with as much love as there is in the whole wide *world*."

Aunt Miranda hugged the disappointed girls. "I'm very grateful to you girls for finding Mystery," she said. "I think we should celebrate. What if you and Mystery and the puppies and I have a sleepover party here Friday night?"

"Hurray!" cheered the girls. "Thanks, Aunt Miranda. That will be great."

"A sleepover party with puppies?" said Emerson, picturing it. "I *love* it! It's *won*derful!"

Chapter 5

Puppy Party

When Friday came, the girls were excited. They surprised Aunt Miranda with a triple-decker cake. The cake was so big that they wheeled it in on a decorated cart. *"Ta-da!"* they said.

"Oh, my!" said Aunt Miranda. "That's the prettiest cake I have ever seen."

After they ate the party refreshments, the girls brushed their teeth and put on their nighties and slippers.

Then Mystery and her puppies made themselves comfortable inside the tent, and the girls made themselves comfortable in their sleeping bags.

"Maybe Shu Ping will let Mystery and the puppies visit us here in the garden when spring comes," said Willa.

Soon the girls—and Mystery and her puppies—were all fast asleep dreaming of spring in the garden.

The next morning, the girls were rolling up their sleeping bags when Aunt Miranda's phone rang. Everything was tidy, and the girls were sitting quietly with the puppies, when she came back.

"That was Shu Ping," Aunt Miranda said. He's home from China, and he's coming over today."

"Oh, no," Ashlyn whispered sadly.

The girls held the puppies closer, dreading the moment they'd have to say good-bye. They looked up at Aunt Miranda with very long faces.

"I told Shu Ping what I told your

parents when I spoke to them last night," said Aunt Miranda. "I explained how hard you tried to find Mystery when she disappeared, and how careful and loving you have been with the puppies." Aunt Miranda smiled. "I said that Mystery trusts you to take good care of her puppies, so they should, too."

The girls were silent. Then Kendall said, "Wait—do you mean . . . ?"

"Yes," said Aunt Miranda, smiling. "Shu Ping and your parents agree. When the puppies are big enough to leave Mystery, you may each take one home."

"Oh, oh, *oh!*" said the girls joyfully. They hugged Aunt Miranda. They hugged each other. They hugged Mystery, whose tail wagged—*thump, thump, thump*—with happiness.

Then, very gently, each happy WellieWisher hugged her puppy—the puppy that was hers to love forever, for her very own.

For Parents

Boredom Busters

When a season begins, it brings a whole slew of new activities for your girl to do, but long weeks of winter sleet and slush or hot summer weather can bring on bouts of boredom. The arrival of Mystery and her puppies was a spectacular solution to the WellieWishers' doldrums! While you may not be able to provide anything quite so exciting, these activities will keep your kids happily occupied if the season starts to drag.

Put on a Talent Show

Just as the WellieWishers made their own fun with a costume guessing game, a talent show is a great way for your girl to channel her creativity and energy. Encourage her to get siblings and friends involved. From picking out costumes to perfecting new talents, she and her pals will be occupied for hours. Show your support by cheering them on when they finally present their show.

Explore the Changing Seasons

Help your girl anticipate the change of seasons and look for clues that are right before her eyes. When you're outside, ask her to look and listen, and then point out telltale signs of change. Can she tell that spring is coming because leaves and flowers are starting to bud? Do ducks or geese migrating south show her that summer is ending and fall is on the way? Is the first frost a wintry hint? Ask your daughter what kind of animal she would like to be and what that animal would be doing to prepare for winter, spring, summer, or fall.

Critter Companions

The WellieWishers each got to take home one of Mystery's puppies, but only after the girls had helped care for them. If your girl has expressed interest in getting a pet, here are some ways to help her develop a sense of responsibility toward animals.

Animal Behavior, Girl Behavior

The WellieWishers learn why Mystery was so sluggish and sleepy earlier in the story when they finally discover Mystery with her puppies. Being attuned to an animal's behavior is a key part of taking good care of it. Talk about what an animal's behavior means, and what the various sounds animals make tell us about how they're feeling. Do they have particular gestures, such as wagging tails or flattened ears, that indicate their mood? How might your girl react to each type of gesture?

Caring for a Pet

Perhaps your family already owns a pet, and your daughter would like to be given more responsibility for it. Together, discuss the animal's needs, such as food, water, grooming, playtime, a place to sleep, and love. Your girl might not be ready to take on sole responsibility for a pet, but she can start to concern herself with the happiness of the family's pet and play a bigger role in its care.

About the Author

VALERIE TRIPP says that she became
a writer because of the kind of person she is.
She says she's curious, and writing requires you
to be interested in everything. Talking is her
favorite sport, and writing is a way of talking
on paper. She's a daydreamer, which helps her
come up with her ideas. And she loves words.
She even loves the struggle to come up
with just the right words as she writes
and rewrites. Ms. Tripp lives in
Maryland with her husband.